The Nymph of the Fountain

By

William Beckford

British Library Cataloguing-in-Publication Data
A catalogue record for this book is available from
the British Library

Contents

WILLIAM BECKFORD

William Thomas Beckford was born in London, England in 1760. At the age of ten, he inherited a vast fortune – consisting of land, cash, and several sugar plantations in Jamaica – from his father, then one of the richest men in England. This gave Beckford the freedom and time to concentrate on his artistic pursuits, including writing. Despite being known in his day primarily as a leading art trader and builder of Fonthill Abbey, Beckford is also remembered for his writing, in particular *Vathek* (1786). The novel, written in French, is notable as one of the early examples of the Gothic genre, and an influence on Mary Shelley's *Frankenstein*. Beckford spent his last years at Lansdown Crescent, before dying there in 1844, aged 84.

AT the distance of three miles from Blackpool in Swabia, there was situated a strong freebooter's hold: it was occupied by a valiant knight, named Siegfried. He was the flower of the free-booting errantry, the scourge of the confederate towns, and the terror of all merchants and carriers, who ventured along the high roads, without purchasing his passport. The moment his vizor was down, his cuirass fixed, his sword girt about his loins, and his golden spurs tinkled at his heels, his heart was steeled to rapine and bloodshed. In conformity with the prejudices of the age, he accounted pillage and plunder among the distinguished privileges of the noblesse: so he fell, from time to time, without mercy, upon the defenceless traders and country people; and be-ing himself muscular and stout, he acknowledged no law but the right of the stronger. At the alarm, 'Siegfried is abroad! Siegfried is at hand!' all Swabia was seized with consternation; the peasants flocked into the fortified towns, and the watchmen upon the towers blew their horns aloud, to give warning of the danger.

But at home, when he had doffed his armour, this dread free-booter became gentle as a lamb, hospitable as an Arab, the kind-est of masters, and the fondest of husbands. His wife was a soft, amiable lady, a perfect pattern of virtue and good conduct. She loved her husband with the most inviolable attachment, and superintended her household with unremitting diligence. When

Siegfried sallied forth in quest of adventures, it was not her custom to sit at the lattice, looking out for admirers, but she set her hand to the wheel, and drew out the flax to a thread so fine, that Arachne herself, the Lydian spinstress, need not have been ashamed to own it. She had brought her husband two daughters, whom she assiduously instructed in the lessons of piety and virtue. In her monastic retirement nothing disturbed her peace of mind, except the unjust means by which her husband acquired his wealth. In her heart she abhorred this privilege of robbery, and she received no satisfaction from his presents of costly stuffs, interwoven with gold and silver. 'Of what use is all this to me, bedewed as it is with the tears of the wronged?' would she say to herself, as she threw it into her coffer, where it was suffered to lie without further notice. She found some relief to these melancholy reflections in administering consolation to the captives, who had fallen into Siegfried's clutches: and numbers from time to time were released in consequence of her mediation; and she never failed to furnish privately with a small sum to bear their expenses home.

At the foot of the eminence on which the castle was seated, a plentiful spring arose within a kind of natural grotto, and immediately concealed itself among the tangled thickets. The fountain-head, according to tradition, was inhabited by a nymph of the family of the Naiads, though, instead of that sort of Grecian appellation, she passed here under the name of the Nicksy. If report spoke true, she had sometimes been seen, on the eve of important occurrences, in the castle. Whenever, during her husband's absence, the noble lady wanted to breathe the fresh air beyond the gloomy walls of the mansion, or steal out to exercise her charity in secret, it was her custom to repair to this fountain. This spot was her favourite retreat. At the grotto she appointed to meet the poor, whom the porter had refused admittance; and here she not only distributed among them the remnants of her table on set days, but also made them considerable presents of money.

Once, when Siegfried had sallied forth with his troop, to waylay the merchants coming from Augspurg fair, he tarried abroad beyond the time he had fixed for his return. His affectionate lady, alarmed at the unprecedented delay, apprehended nothing less than that he had been slain in the encounter, or at least had fallen into the enemy's hand. Hope and fear wrestled in her bosom for several days. She would often call out to the dwarf that kept watch upon the battlements: 'Look out, Hansel, towards the wood, and see what makes such a rustling among the trees. – Hark! I hear a trampling of horses in the valley! – What raises yonder cloud of dust? – Dost thou espy thy master hastening home?' Hansel mournfully replied, 'There is nothing stirring in the wood – I hear no trampling of horses in the valley – I see no clouds of dust rising – there is no nodding of plumes afar off.' She repeated these inquiries incessantly, till the evening star began to twinkle, and the full moon peeped over the eastern hills. Being no longer able to endure her apartment, she threw her cloak over her shoulders, and stole out at the private door towards the grove of beeches, that she might pursue her melancholy ideas without interruption, beside her favourite fountain. Her eye was dissolved in tears, and her moans harmonized with the melting murmurs of the rivulet, as it lost itself among the thick grass.

As she approached the grotto, it seemed as if an airy phantom hovered just within the entrance; but she was too deeply absorbed in sorrow to pay much attention to the vision; and a transitory idea, that it was some illusion of the moonlight, passed half unperceived across her imagination. But on a nearer approach a figure in white was distinctly seen to move, and to beckon her into the grove. An involuntary horror fell upon the mournful lady, but she did not fly back; she only stopped short to take a more distinct view. The report concerning the inhabitant of the spring, that circulated in the neighbourhood, had not failed to reach her ears, and she now recognized the phantom in white for the nymph of the fountain. She concluded that the apparition denoted some important family event: and her husband being uppermost in her thoughts, she instantly began to tear her raven locks, and set up a loud lamentation, 'Alas, unhappy day! Ah, Siegfried, Siegfried, thou art no more! – Woe is me, thou art cold and stiff! – Thou hast made me a widow, and thy poor children are become orphans!'

While she lamented in this manner, wringing her hands and beating her bosom, a gentle voice was heard to proceed from the grotto: 'Be not afflicted Matilda; I do not come to announce bad tidings: approach without fear; I am only a friend that wishes to converse with you.' The appearance and address of the Naiad were so little alarming, that the noble lady did not hesitate to comply with the invitation. As she stepped into the grotto, the inhabitant took her kindly by the hand, kissed her forehead, seated herself close beside her, and spake: 'Welcome to my habitation, beloved mortal, whose heart is pure as the water of my fountain: therefore the invisible powers are all propitious to thee. As for me, the only favour I can confer upon thee is to disclose the fortunes of thy life. Thy husband is safe: ere the morning cock crows thou shalt fold him in thy arms. Do not be apprehensive of mourning for thy husband, the spring of thy life shall be dried up before his. But thou must first bear a daughter in an eventful hour. The balance of her fate is equally posed between happiness and misery. The stars are not unpropitious, but an unfriendly gleam threatens to rob her of a mother's fostering care.'

The tender-hearted Matilda was greatly affected, when she heard that her daughter was to become an infant orphan. She was unable to suppress her maternal tears. The Naiad, deeply touched by her sorrow, endeavoured to compose her mind: 'Be not afflicted beyond measure; when thou art no longer able to tend thy infant, I will myself discharge a mother's office, on condition, however, that I am chosen for one of her godmothers, that I may have some interest in the babe. Be careful at the same time that the child, provided thou wilt entrust her to me, brings me back safe the baptismal gift which I shall leave with her.' This was no offer to be rejected: to ratify the treaty, the Naiad took a smooth pebble out of the rivulet, and gave it to Matilda; charging her, at the proper season, to send one of her damsels to throw it onto the fountainhead, when she would consider it as a summons to attend the ceremony. The matron promised that her injunction should be punctually observed, laid all these things up in her heart, and returned to the castle. Her Naiad patroness stepped into the water, and vanished.

Not long afterwards the dwarf blew a merry blast with his horn from the watchtower; and Siegfried, with his horsemen and a rich booty, entered the courtyard. Before a year had expired, the virtuous lady communicated to her lord a discovery, which raised in his mind the pleasing expectation of the arrival of an heir male. It cost Matilda much reflection, before she could contrive how to manage about the Nymph of the Fountain, for many reasons restrained her from communicating the adventure at the grove to her husband. About the same time it happened that Siegfried received a message of mortal defiance from a knight whom he had offended at a feast. He lost no time in equipping himself and his squires, and when, according to his custom, he came to bid his wife farewell, just before he mounted, she eagerly inquired into the nature of his design; and when, instead of satisfying her, he affectionately reproved her for her unusual and ill-timed curiosity, she covered her face and wept bitterly. Her tears melted the knight's generous heart nevertheless he tore himself away, and, without showing any signs of sympathy, rode briskly to the place of rendezvous, where, after a severe conflict, he dismounted his adversary, and returned in triumph.

His faithful spouse received him with open arms: and by endearing conversation, and all the artillery of female address, strove to extort a communication of his late adventure. But he constantly barricaded every avenue to his heart by the bolt of insensibility, and all her artifices were unavailing. Finding that she still persisted in her purpose, he endeavoured to abash her by raillery; – 'Good grandmother Eve, thy daughters have not degenerated: prying curiosity has continued to be the portion of woman to the present day; not one but would have longed for the forbidden fruit.' 'I beg your pardon, my dear husband,' replied the artful dame; 'you are too partial to the ladies; there is not a man existing who has not received his lawful portion of mother Eve's inheritance; the whole difference consists in this, the loving wife neither has, nor is permitted to have a secret from her husband. Could I find it in my heart to conceal anything from you, I would risk a great wager that you would never be at rest till you had drawn the secret from me.' 'And I assure you, upon my honour,' replied he, 'that your secret would never give me a moment's uneasiness – nay, you may make the trial, I give you my full consent.' This was just the point to which Matilda desired to bring her husband: 'Well then,' said she, 'you know, my dear, that my time is fast approaching. You shall allow me to choose one of the godmothers. I design this office for a dear friend, whom I have locked up in my heart, but with whom you are altogether unacquainted. I only desire that you will never press me to tell who she is, whence she comes, nor where she lives. If you promise this, and keep steady to the obligation, I will consent to lose the wager, and willingly own that the firmness of imperial man has a right to triumph over the frailty of our sex.' Siegfried, without scruple, engaged his honour to forbear all inquiry; and Matilda secretly rejoiced at the success of her strategem.

In a few weeks she presented her husband with a daughter. The father would much rather have taken a boy into his arms; he nevertheless rode about in high spirits to invite his friends and neighbours to the christening. They all appeared on the appointed day; and when the lady heard the rolling of carriages, the neighing of horses, and the hum of a large company, she called to her one of her trusty maids, and charged her, 'Take this pebble; go and throw it behind you, without saying a word, into the fountain in the grotto: be careful to do exactly as I have directed you.' The maid punctually obeyed the injunction; and before she returned, an unknown lady stepped into the apartment where the company was assembled, and made her obeisance very gracefully to the knights and dames. When the child was brought out, and the priest had gone up to the font, the highest place fell to the stranger, every one respectfully making way for her. Her beauty, and the gracefulness of her demeanour attracted every eye; and above all the splendour of her dress, which consisted of a flowing gown of azure blue silk, with cuffs turned up with white satin; she was, moreover, as heavily laden with pearls and jewels as my Lady of Loretto on her transparent veil, which flowed in easy folds from the crown of the head, over her shoulders, down to her heels: and the tip of the veil was dripping wet, as if it had been drawn through water.

The unknown lady, by her unexpected appearance, had so disarranged the groupe, that they forgot to ask for instructions about the child's name; so the priest christened it Matilda, after its mother. After the ceremony, little Matilda was carried back to her mother, and the ladies followed in order to congratulate the new-made mother, and bestow upon their god-daughter the accustomed baptismal boon. At sight of the stranger Matilda betrayed some emotion. She probably felt a mixture of pleasure and surprise, at the punctuality shewn by the Naiad in the performance of her engagement. She cast a stolen glance at her husband, who replied by a smile, which none of the bystanders could decypher, and afterwards affected to take no notice of the stranger. The presents now engaged all the mother's attention: a shower of gold was poured upon the nursling from the liberal hands of its sponsors. Last of all, the unknown lady came forward with her boon, and much disappointed the expectations of her associates. They looked for a present of inestimable value from so splendid a personage, especially when they saw her produce, and unfold with great care and method, a silk case, which, as it turned out, contained nothing but a musk-ball, and that not the precious drug, but an imitation, turned in box-wood. – This she laid very gravely upon the cradle, and gave the mother a friendly kiss upon the forehead, and then quitted the apartment.

So paltry a present occasioned a loud whisper through the room, and a laugh of scorn succeeded. Several shrewd remarks and sly allusions – for the festivity of a christening has in all ages been remarkable for its effect in brightening the wit – entertained the guests at the expense of the fair stranger. But, as the knight and his lady observed a mysterious silence upon the subject, both the curious and voluble were obliged to rest satisfied with distant conjectures. No more was seen of the stranger, nor could anyone tell which way she had vanished. Siegfried was secretly tormented to know who the lady with the dripping veil, for so, for want of a better name, was she entitled, might be. His tongue, however, was bound by the dread of falling into a woman's weakness, and by the inviolable sanctity of his knightly word. Nevertheless, in the moment of matrimonial confidence, the question, 'Tell me now, my dear, who was the lady with the dripping veil,' often was ready to bolt. He expected one day or other a full gratification of his curiosity by dint of cunning or caresses, firmly relying on that property of the female heart, in consequence of which it is as little able to keep a secret as a sieve of holding water. For this time, however, he was mistaken in his calculation. Matilda kept the bridle on her tongue, and laid up the riddle in her heart with no less care than the musk-ball in her casket of jewels.

Ere the infant had outgrown the leading-strings, the nymph's prophecy respecting her affectionate mother was fulfilled; she was taken ill, and died so suddenly, that she had not even time to think of the musk-ball, much less could she dispose of it for the advantage of little Matilda, according to the directions of her patroness. Siegfried was unfortunately absent at a tournament at Augspurg, and was on his way homeward as this melancholy event happened, with his heart bounding for joy, on account of a prize he had received from the hands of the Emperor Frederick himself. As soon as the dwarf on the watchtower was aware of his lord's approach, he blew his horn, as usual, to announce his arrival to the people in the castle; but he did not blow a cheerful note, as on former occasions. The mournful blast smote the knight's heart sore, and raised up sad apprehensions in his breast: 'Alas!' he cries, 'do you hear those doleful sounds? It is more ungrateful to my ears than the screech-owl's screaming. Hansel proclaims nothing good: I fear it is a death's blast.' The squires were all dumb with apprehension, they looked their master sorrowfully in the face; at last one took up the word, and spake, 'There goes a single raven croaking to our left hand – Heaven defend us! for I am afraid there is a corpse in the house.' The knight upon this clapped spurs to his horse, and galloped over the heath till the sparks flew amain. The drawbridge fell; he cast an eager look into the courtyard, where he beheld the symbol of a dead body set out before the door; it consisted of a lantern crowned with a flag of crape, and with a light; moreover all the window-shutters were closed. At the same instant he heard the lamentation of the household, for they had just placed Matilda's coffin on the bier. At the head sat the two elder daughters, all covered with crape and frize. They were silently shedding showers of tears over their departed mother. The youngest was seated at the foot; she was as yet incapable of feeling her loss, and so she was employed in stripping, with childish unconcern, the flowers that were strewed over the dead body. This melancholy spectacle was too much for Siegfried's firmness: he began to sob and lament aloud, fell upon the ice-cold corpse, bedewed the wan cheeks with his tears, pressed with his quivering lips against the pale mouth, and gave himself up, without reserve, to the bitterness of sorrow. Having laid up his armour in the armoury, he drew his hat deep over his eyes, put on a black mourning cloak, and took his place beside the bier, brooding over his affliction; and at length conferred on his deceased wife the last honours of a solemn funeral.

It has been remarked by a certain great wit, that the most violent feelings are always the shortest in their duration. Accordingly the knight, bowed as he had been to the ground, felt the load of sorrow grow lighter by degrees, and in a short time entertained serious thoughts of repairing his loss by a second wife. The lot of his choice fell upon a brisk young damsel, the very antitype of the gentle Matilda. The household of course soon put on a different form. The new lady delighted in pomp and parade; her extravagance knew no bounds, and she comported herself haughtily towards the domestics; she held banquets and carousals without number; her fruitfulness peopled the house with a numerous progeny. The daughters of the first marriage were disregarded, and they very soon were put out of sight and out of mind. The two elder sisters were placed in a religious establishment in Germany. Little Matilda was banished to a remote corner of the house, and placed under the superintendance of a nurse, that she might no more intrude upon her stepmother's notice. As this vain woman was utterly averse to all household affairs, her want of economy rose to such a pitch, that the revenues arising from club-law were inadequate to the expenses, although the knight stretched his privilege to the utmost. My lady found herself frequently under the necessity of despoiling the repositories of her predecessor. She was obliged to barter away the rich stuffs, or surrender them on pawn to the Jews. Happening one day to be in great household distress, she rummaged every drawer and coffer for valuables; in her search, she stumbled upon a private compartment in an old escrutoire, and, to her great joy, among other articles, fell upon Matilda's casket of jewels. Her greedy eye devoured the sparkling diamond rings, the ear-pendants, bracelets, necklaces, lockets, and the whole trinkets besides. She took an accurate inventory of the whole stock, examined article by article, and calculated in idea, how much this glorious windfall would produce. Among other rarities she was aware of the wooden musk-ball; she tried to unscrew it, but it was swelled by the damp. She then poised it on her hand, but finding it as light as a hollow nut, she concluded it was an empty ring-case, and tossed it as if worthless lumber out at the window.

Little Matilda happened to be playing on the grass-plot immediately below. Seeing a round body roll along the turf, she grasped with a child's eagerness at the new plaything; nor was she a whit less delighted at this, than her mother-in-law at the other prize. It afforded her amusement for several days; she was so fond of it, that she would not part with it out of her own hands. One sultry summer's noon, the nurse carried her charge to the grotto for coolness; the child, after a while, asked for her afternoon's cake; but the nurse had forgotten to bring it, and did not chuse to be at the trouble of going back quite to the house: so, to keep the little one quiet, she went among the bushes to pluck a handful of blackberries. The child meanwhile played with the musk-ball, rolling it before her and running after it: once she rolled it a little too far, and the child's joy, in the strictest sense, tumbled into the water. Immediately a female, fresh as the morning, beautiful as an angel, and smiling like one of the Graces, appeared in view. The child started, for at first she supposed it was her stepmother, in whose way she never came without a beating or a scolding. But the Nymph accosted her in the most engaging terms: 'Be not afraid, my little dear, I am thy godmamma: come to me: look, here is thy plaything that fell into the water.' The sight of this enticed the child towards her: the Nymph took her up in her arms, pressed her gently to her bosom, kissed her affectionately, and bedewed her face with tears. 'Poor little orphan,' said she, 'I have promised to be instead of a mother to thee, and I will keep my word. Come often here to see me. Thou wilt always find me in this grotto upon throwing a pebble into the fountainhead. Keep thy musk-ball with the utmost care: be sure, never play with it any more, lest thou lose it; for some time or other, it will fulfil three of thy wishes. When thou art grown a little older, I will tell thee more. At present thou wouldst not understand me.' She gave her much good advice besides, suitable to her tender age, and, above all things, enjoined her silence. Soon afterwards the nurse returned, and the Nymph was gone.

Matilda was a sensible, intelligent child; and she had reflection enough to hold her tongue on the subject of godmamma Nicksy. At her return to the castle, she asked for needle and thread, which she used for the purpose of sewing the musk-ball in the lower tuck of her frock. All her thoughts are now turned towards the fountain. Whenever the weather permitted, she proposed a walk there: her superintendant could deny nothing to the coaxing little maid; and, as she seemed to inherit this predilection, the grotto having always been the favourite retreat of her mother, she gratified her wishes so much the more cheerfully. Matilda always contrived some pretext for sending away the nurse; no sooner was her back fairly turned, than she dropped a pebble into the spring, which instantly procured her the company of her indulgent godmother. In a few revolutions of the year, the little orphan attained the age of puberty: her charms disclosed themselves as the bud of a rose opens its hundred leaves, opens in modest dignity amid the many-coloured race of vulgar flowers. She blossomed indeed but in the kitchen-garden; for she lived unnoticed among the servants, she was never suffered to appear at her stepmother's voluptuous banquets, but was confined to her chamber, where she employed herself in needle-work; and at the close of the day found, in the society of the Nymph of the Fountain, ample compensation for the noisy pleasures of which she was deprived. The Naiad was not only her companion and confidante, but likewise her instructress in every female accomplishment; and she was studious to form her exactly after the pattern of her virtuous mother.

One day the Nymph redoubled her tenderness: she clasped the charming Matilda in her arms, reclined her head upon her shoulder, and displayed so much melancholy fondness, that the young lady could not refrain from letting fall some sympathizing tears upon her hand, as she pressed it in silence against her lips. The Naiad appeared still more afflicted at this correspondence of feeling; 'Alas! my child,' said she, in a mournful voice, 'thou weepest, and knowest not wherefore; but thy tears are ominous of thy fate. A sad revolution awaits yon fortress upon the hill. Ere the mower whets his scythe, or the west wind whistles over the stubble of the wheat field, all shall be desolate and forlorn. When the maidens of the castle go forth, at the hour of twilight, to fetch water from my spring, and return with empty pitchers, then remember that the calamity is at hand. Preserve carefully the musk-ball, which will fulfil three of the wishes, but do not squander away this privilege heedlessly. Fare thee well; we meet no more at this spot.' She then instructed her ward in another magic property of the ball, which might be serviceable in time of need. At length her tears and sobs stifled her voice, and she was no more seen. One evening, about the season of corn harvest, the maids that went out for water returned pale and affrighted, with their pitchers empty; their teeth chattered, and every limb quivered as if they were shaken by the shivering fit of an ague. 'The lady in white,' they reported, 'is sitting beside the well, uttering deep sighs, and wringing her hands in great affliction.' Of this evil omen most of the squires armour-bearers made mock, declaring it to be all illusion and women's prate. Curiosity, however, carried several out to examine whether the report was true or false. They saw the same apparition; nevertheless they mustered up courage to approach the fountain, but as they came near the phantom was gone. Many interpretations were attempted, but no one fell upon the true import of the sign; Matilda alone was privy to it; but she held her peace, in compliance with the strenuous injunction of the Naiad. She repaired, dejected, to her chamber, where she sat alone, in fearful expectation of the things that were to come to pass.

Siegfried of Blackpool had degenerated by this time into a mere woman's tool: he could never satisfy his spend thrift wife with enough of robbery and plunder. When he was not abroad waylaying travellers, she prepared a feast, invited a number of bacchanalian comrades, and kept him in a continued fit of intoxication, that he might not perceive the decay of his household. When there was a want of money or provisions, Jacob Fugger's broad-wheeled wagons, or the rich bales of the Venetians, afforded a never failing resource. Outraged at these continual depredations, the general congress of the Swabian alliance determined upon Siegfried's destruction, since remonstrances and admonitions were of no avail. Before he would believe they were in right earnest, the banners of the confederates were displayed before his castle-gate, and nothing was left him but the resolution to sell his life as dear as possible. The guns shattered the bastions: on both sides the cross-bowmen did their utmost; it hailed bolts and arrows: a shaft, discharged in a luckless moment, when Siegfried's protecting angel had stepped aside, pierced his vizor, and lodged deep in his brain. Great dismay fell upon his party at the loss of their undaunted leader: the cowardly hoisted a white flag; the courageous tore it down again from the tower: the enemy, concluding, from these appearances, that discord and confusion prevailed within the fort, seized the opportunity for making the assault; they clambered over the walls, carried the gates, let down the drawbridge, and smote every living thing that came in the way with the edge of their sword: they did not spare even the extravagant wife, the author of the calamity, nor her helpless children, for the allies were as much exasperated against the freebooting nobility, as the French mob against their feudal seigneurs, since the fall of despotism. The castle was ransacked, then set on fire and levelled with the ground, so that not one stone was left on another.

During the alarm of the siege, Matilda barricaded the door of her apartment in the best manner she was able, and took post at her little window in the roof of her house; and having observed the issue of the affair from this advantageous station, and finding that bolts and bars were not likely to afford her any farther security, she put on her veil, and then turned her musk-ball thrice round, at the same time repeating the words her friend the Naiad had taught her:

> Behind me, night, before me, day,
> That none behold my secret way.

She now came down stairs in perfect confidence, and passed unperceived through the confusion of slaughter. She did not quit her paternal residence without deep sorrow of heart, which was much aggravated by her being utterly at a loss which way to take. She hastened from the scene of carnage and desolation, till her delicate feet absolutely refused to serve her any longer. The falling of night, together with extreme weariness, constrained her to take up her lodging at the foot of an oak, in the open fields. As soon as she had seated herself on the cold turf, her tears began to flow, and she made no attempt to restrain them. She turned aside her head to take a farewell view, and to breathe her last blessing on the place where she had passed the years of her childhood. As she lifted her eyes, behold the sky appeared all blood-red: from this sign she concluded that the residence of her forefathers had become a prey to the flames. She turned away her face from this horrid spectacle, heartily wishing for the hour when the sparkling stars should grow dim, and the dawn peep from the east. Ere the morning dew had settled in big round tears on the grass, she proceeded on her wandering pilgrimage. She arrived betimes at her village, where a compassionate housewife took her in, and recruited her strength with a slice of bread and a bowl of milk. With this woman she bartered her clothes in exchange for meaner apparel, and then joined a company of carriers on their way to Augspurg. In her forlorn situation, she had no other resource than to seek a place in some family: but, as it was not the season for hiring servants, it was a long time before she could find employment.

Count Conrad of Swabeck, a knight of the order of knights templars, chancellor and champion of the diocese of Augspurg, had a palace in that city, where he usually resided in winter. During his absence Gertrude, the housekeeper, bore sovereign sway in the mansion. Gertrude, like many other worthy persons of her sex and calling, had engrafted the failing of an inexorable scold upon the virtue of unremitting industry. Her failing was so much more notorious throughout the city, than her virtue, that few servants offered their services, and none had been able to stay out their time with her. She raised such an alarm, wherever she moved, that the maids dreaded the rattling of her keys as much as children do hobgoblins. Saucepans and heads suffered alike for her ill-humours; when no projectiles were within reach, she would wield her bunch of keys in her brawny arm, and beat the sides and shoulders of her subalterns black and blue. Every description of an ill-conditioned woman was summed up with, 'in short, she is as bad as Gertrude, the Count's housekeeper.' One day she had administered her office of correction so rigorously, that all the household decamped with one consent: it was at this conjuncture that the gentle Matilda approached to offer her services. But she had taken care to conceal her elegant shape, by fastening a large lump on her left shoulder as if she had been crooked; her beautiful auburn hair was covered with a large coarse cap; and she had anointed her face and hands, in imitation of the gipsies, with juice of walnut husks. Mother Gertrude, who, on hearing the bell ring, poked her head out at the window, was no sooner aware of the singular figure at the door, than she exclaimed, in her shrill tone, 'Go, get about your business, hussy: there is nothing for great idle girls, like you, here; such sluts should be in the house of correction!' After this salutation she hastily shut the window.

Matilda was not to be so easily repulsed. She rang till the Megara's head was a second time protruded from the casement, for the purpose of retorting upon this insolence of perseverance a torrent of abuse. But before she could unfold her toothless jaws, the young lady had declared her business. — 'Who art thou?' demanded the head from above, 'Whence dost thou come? And what canst thou do?' — The supposed gipsy answered:

> 'I am an orphan, Matilda by name:
> I'm a stout girl and nimble,
> An manage the thimble;
> Can spin, card, and knit,
> And handle the spit;
> I can stew, bake, and brew;
> Am honest and true,
> And here to serve you.'

The housekeeper, softened by the whimsical recitative of all these important qualifications, opened her door to the nut brown virgin, and gave her a shilling in earnest, as kitchen-maid. The new hireling plied her business so diligently, that Gertrude, for want of practice, lost her dexterity at hurling saucepans at a mark. She still, however, retained her morose and querulous humour; and was sure to find fault with everything. Nevertheless her subaltern, by avoiding all contradiction, by gentleness and patience, saved herself many effusions of ill-humour.

About the falling of the first snow, the housekeeper had the whole mansion swept and scoured, the cobwebs brushed, the windows washed, the floors sanded, the shutters opened, and every thing put in readiness for the reception of her lord, who soon afterwards made his appearance, followed by a long train of servants, a troop of horses, and a loud cry of hounds. The arrival of the Templar raised little curiosity in Matilda; her work in the kitchen had grown so upon her hands, that she had not a moment to gape after him. One morning, as she was drawing water at the well, he accidentally passed by her, and his appearance kindled sensations in her bosom to which it had hitherto been an entire stranger. She beheld a young man, whose beauty exceeded the fairest of her dreams. The sparkling of his eye, the good-humour that lightened up his features, his flowing hair, half concealed by the plumes that over-shadowed his soldier's hat, his firm step, and the grace of his whole demeanour, acted so powerfully on her heart, that the blood moved with increasing velocity along her veins. She now, for the first time, felt the degraded station to which an untoward fate had reduced her, and this sentiment was a heavier load than the large pitcher. She returned, deeply musing to the kitchen, and, for the first time since she had begun to exercise her culinary functions, over-salted all the soup, an oversight which drew down upon her a severe reprimand from the housekeeper. The handsome knight hovered before her imagination day and night: she was continually longing to see him; and whenever she heard the sound of his spurs, as he crossed the courtyard, she was sure to discover a want of water in the kitchen, and ran with the pitcher in her hand to the well; though the stately cavalier never once condescended to bestow a glance upon her.

Count Conrad seemed to exist merely for the purpose of pleasure. He attended every banquet and rejoicing in the city, which, from its commerce with the Venetians, was become rich and luxurious. One day there was a tilting-match at the ring: the next a tournament; the third a mayor's feast. Nor was there any scarcity of dances at the town hall, and in every street. Here the noblemen toyed and frolicked with the citizens' daughters; occasionally presenting them with gold rings and silken stuffs. By carnival-time this tumult of dissipation had arisen to its highest pitch, but Matilda had no share in the festivity: she sat all day in the smoky kitchen, and wept till her pining eyes became sore, constantly bewailing the caprice of fortune, which heaps a profusion of the joy of life over her favourites, while from others she greedily snatches every instant of cheerfulness. Her heart was heavy she knew not why; for she had no suspicion that love had taken up his abode there. This restless inmate, who throws every house where he lodges into confusion, whispered everyday a thousand romantic schemes into her head, and every night busied her fancy with bewitching dreams. She was now walking arm in arm with the Templar in a delicious garden: now she was immured in the sanctuary of the cloister; the Count was standing at the grate, longing to converse with her, but the strict abbess would not grant permission: sometimes he was leading her out to open a festive dance. These enchanting dreams were very often suddenly cut short by the jingling of Mother Gertrude's bunch of keys, with which it was her custom to rouse the sleeping household betimes. However the ideas spun by imagination during the night, served to amuse her thoughts by day.

Love knows no dangers; the enamoured Matilda formed project after project, till at last she fell upon a scheme to realize the fondest of her dreams. She had still her godmother the Naiad's musk-ball safe: she had never felt any desire to open it, and make an essay of its power to gratify her wishes. She now resolved to try the experiment. The citizens of Augspurg had, about this time, prepared a sumptuous banquet, in compliment to the Emperor Frederic, on the birth of his son, Prince Maximilian. The rejoicings were to continue three days. Innumerable nobles and prelates were invited. Each day there was a tournament, and a rich prize for the victor: each evening the most beautiful damsels danced with the knights till break of day. Count Conrad did not fail to attend these festivities; each time he was the favourite of the matrons and virgins. No one, indeed, could hope to share his lawful love, for he was Templar; nevertheless he was the object of all their good wishes – he was so handsome, and danced so charmingly.

Matilda had come to the resolution of sallying forth in quest of adventures, on this occasion. After she had arranged the kitchen, and everything was quiet in the house, she retired to her bedchamber, and, washing away the tawny varnish with sweet-scented soap, called the lilies and roses of her complexion into new bloom. She then took the musk-ball into her hand, and wished for a new gown, as rich and elegant as fancy could form, with all its appurtenances. On screwing off the top, a piece of silk issued out, expanding itself, and rustling all the while, as if a stream of water was gushing on her lap. On examination it proved a full dress, fitted up with every little article: the gown fitted as exactly as if it had been cast on her body. – While she was putting it on, she felt that internal exultation, which girls always experience when they adorn themselves for the sake of the other sex, and spread out their dangerous meshes. Her vanity was fully gratified, as she took a survey of her dress, and she was perfectly content with herself. Accordingly she did not defer a moment longer the execution of her stratagem. She thrice whirled round the magic ball, saying,

> In sleep profound,
> Each eye be drown'd.

Instantly a deep slumber fell upon all the household, not excepting the vigilant housekeeper and the Janus at the door. Matilda glided in a moment out of the house, passed unseen along the streets, and stepped into the ballroom with the air of one of the Graces. The charming new figure raised great admiration among the company; and along the lofty gallery which encircled the ballroom there arose a general whisper. Some admired the elegance of the stranger's person, others the fashion of her dress, others inquired who she was, and whence she came; but on these points no one could satisfy his neighbour's curiosity. Among the noble knights, who crowded to take a peep at the unknown damsel, the Templar was far from hindmost. He was by no means a woman hater; and, though an exact connoisseur in the sex, he thought he had never seen a sweeter person nor a more happy countenance. He approached, and engaged her to dance. She modestly presented her hand, and danced with enchanting elegance. Her nimble feet scarce touched the floor, and the ease and gracefulness of her movements set every eye in rapture. Count Conrad paid his heart for his partner. He no more quitted the fair dancer. He said as many fine things and pushed his suit with as much zeal and earnestness, as the most enamoured of our heroes of romance, for whom the world becomes too narrow a stage, the moment they are goaded on by malicious Cupid. Matilda was as little mistress of her own heart: she conquered, and was vanquished in her turn. Her first essay in love was crowned with success equal to her fondest wishes. It was not in her power to keep the sympathy of her feelings concealed beneath the cloak of female reserve. The enraptured knight soon perceived that he was no hopeless lover; his chief anxiety arose from his entire ignorance of his charming partner; and how to prosecute his suit, unless he could discover where she lived. But on this subject all inquiries were in vain: she eluded every question, and after all his efforts he could only obtain a promise that she would make her appearance at the next night's ball. He thought to outwit her, in case she should forfeit her word, by posting all his servants to watch her home, for he supposed her to be of Augspurg, while the company, from his unremitting attention, concluded she was a lady of the Count's acquaintance.

The dawn had already peeped, before she could find an opportunity of slipping away from the knight, and quitting the room. But no sooner had she passed the door, than she turned her musk-ball thrice round, and repeated the spell:

> Behind me, night, before me, day,
> That none behold my secret way.

By these means she got to her chamber, in spite of the Baron's sentinels, who did not catch a glimpse of her, though they were hovering in every street. No sooner had she shut the door behind her, than she locked up the silken apparel safe in her box, put on her greasy cook's dress, and resumed her ordinary occupations. The old housekeeper, who had been rattling up the rest of the servants with her bunch of keys, finding Matilda stirring so early, bestowed an ungracious compliment on her diligence.

Never had any day appeared so tedious to the knight as that which succeeded the ball. Every hour seemed a week: his heart was in perpetual agitation between longing impatience and apprehension, lest the inscrutable beauty should fail in her engagement, for Suspicion, the train-bearer of Love, allowed his thoughts as little repose as the wind did the flag that was flying on the tower. At the approach of evening he equipped himself for the ball, with greater magnificence than the preceding day; the three golden rings the ancient badge of nobility, all beset with diamonds, sparkled in the front of his dress. He was the

first at the rendezvous of pleasure, where, having stationed himself so as to command the entrance, he scrutinized everyone who
came in with the keen eyes of an eagle, expecting, with all the
eagerness of impatience, the arrival of his dulcinea. The evening
star was already advanced high in the horizon, before the young
lady could find time to retire to her chamber, and consider what
she should do: whether she should extort a second wish from
the musk-ball, or reserve it for some more important occurrence
of life. The faithful counsellor, Reason, advised the latter; but
Love enjoined the former with such impetuosity, that Reason
was quite silenced, and soon withdrew altogether. Matilda
wished for a dress of rose-coloured satin, most sumptuously be-
decked with jewels. The complaisant musk-ball exerted its
powers: the apparel exceeded the lady's expectation; she per-
formed, in high spirits, the rites of the toilette, and, by the help
of the talisman, arrived at the spot where she was so ardently expected, without having been beheld by mortal eye. She appeared
far more charming than before. The heart of Conrad bounded
for joy at the first glimpse of her person. A power, as irresistible
as the central attraction of the globe, hurried him towards her
through the vortex of dancers; and as he had now almost given
up all hopes of seeing her again, he was unable to breathe forth
the effusions of his gladness. In order to gain time to recover
himself, and to hide his confusion, he led her out to dance,
when every couple immediately made way for the charming
pair. The beautiful stranger, hand in hand with the noble
knight, floated along, light as the goddess of spring upon the
pinion of Zephyr.

At the conclusion of the dance, Count Conrad conducted his
partner into the contiguous apartment, under the pretext of of-
fering her some refreshment. Here, in the tone of a well-bred
courtier, he said a thousand flattering things, as he had done the
day before; but the cold language of politeness insensibly kindl-
ing into the language of the heart terminated in a passionate
and earnest declaration of love. Matilda hearkened with bash-
ful gladness: her beating heart and glowing cheeks betrayed
her inward emotions; and when she was pressed for a verbal

declaration, she modestly said: 'I am not displeased, noble knight, with what you have expressed of affection both today and before: I am unwilling to believe that your purpose is to deceive me by false insinuations. But how can I participate of the wedded love of a Templar, who must have taken the vow of perpetual celibacy. Solve me this paradox, or you will find that you might as well have uttered your smooth language to the winds: therefore explain without disguise how we may be united according to the rites of holy mother church, that so our marriage may abide in the sight of God and man.'

The knight answered seriously and without guile: 'You speak as becomes a discreet and virtuous maiden; I will therefore solve your difficulty without fraud or deceit, and satisfy your question. You must know that at the time of my reception into the order my brother William, the heir of the family was alive. Since his decease I have obtained a dispensation from my vow, as the last remaining branch of the house, and am at liberty to quit the profession of knighthood whenever I please. But never till the moment I saw you, has almighty love taken possession of my heart: from that instant I felt an entire change within my bosom; and I finally persuaded that you, and no other, are allotted me by Heaven as my wedded bride. If therefore you do not refuse me your hand, nothing from this moment forwards but death shall part us.' 'Consider well what you propose,' replied Matilda, 'lest repentance overtake you. Those who marry in haste, have commonly leisure to repent. I am an entire stranger: you know nothing of my rank or station; whether I am your equal in birth and dignity, or whether a borrowed lustre dazzles your eyes. It is unbecoming a man of your rank to promise anything lightly: but a nobleman's engagements should be held inviolable.' Here Count Conrad eagerly seized her hand, pressed it close to his heart, and in the warmth of his affection exclaimed, 'Yes, I pledge my knightly honour, and engage my soul's salvation, were you the meanest man's daughter, and but a pure and undefiled virgin, I will receive you for my wedded wife, and raise you to high honour.'

On this he pulled a diamond ring from his finger, and gave it her as the pledge of his truth; and took in return the first kiss from her chaste untasted lips, and thus proceeded: 'That you may entertain no suspicion of my purpose, I invite you three days hence to my house, ·where I will appoint my friends, — knights, nobles, and prelates, — to be witness to our union.'

Matilda resisted this proposal with all her might: she was not satisfied at the galloping rate at which the knight's love proceeded; but determined to prove the constancy of his affection. He did not cease to press her to consent, but she said neither no or yes. The company did not break up before the dawn of day. Matilda vanished; and the knight, who had not enjoyed one wink of sleep, summoned the vigilant housekeeper betimes, and gave her orders to prepare a sumptuous feast.

As the dread skeleton figure with the scythe traverses palaces and cottages, mowing down whatever falls in his way, so old Gertrude, having her inexorable fist armed with the slaughtering knife, paced through the poultry-yard and hen-pens, dispensing life and death among the domestic fowls. The unsuspecting tenants of the court fell by dozens before her burnished blade, flapped their wings in agony for the last time, and hens, doves, and stupid capons, yielded up their lives in heaps. Matilda had so many fowls to pluck, draw, and skewer, that she was obliged to give up her night's rest: yet she did not grudge her labour, well knowing that the banquet was all on her account. The hour approached; the cheerful host flew to receive every guest as he arrived, and every time the knocker sounded, he imagined the beautiful stranger was at the door: but when it was opened, some reverend prelate's paunch, matron's gravity, or solemn office-bearer's visage, strutted in. Though the guests were assembled, the server lingered long before he served up the dishes. Sir Conrad still waited for the charming bride; but at last, when she did not appear, he was reluctantly obliged to give the signal for dinner. When the guests were seated, there appeared one cover too much; but no one could guess who it was that had dishonoured the knight's invitation. The founder of the feast lost his cheerfulness by perceptible gradations, and in spite of all his exertions it was not in his power to enliven his guests with the spirit of mirth. The leaven of spleen soon soured the sweet cake of social joy, and in the banqueting room there prevailed a silence as dead as at a funeral feast. The musicians who had been summoned for the evening ball, were discharged; and for this time the banquet ended without one tuneful sound, in the house that had always before been the mansion of joy.

The disconcerted guests stole away at an unusually early hour: the knight longed for the solitude of his bedchamber; he was impatient for an opportunity to ruminate at liberty on the fickleness of love. While his reflections were engaged by the melancholy subject, he tossed and tumbled to and fro on his bed: with the most intense exertion of thought, he could not determine what conclusion to draw from the absence of his mistress. The blood boiled in his veins; and ere he had closed an eye, the sun peeped in through his curtains. The servants found their master in a violent paroxyism of fever, wrestling with wild fancies. This discovery threw the whole family into the most violent consternation: the men of medicine tripped up and down stairs, exhibited solemn faces, and wrote recipes by the yard: in the apothecary's shop the mortars were all set going as if they had been chiming for morning prayer. But not one of the physicians fell upon the herb Eye-balm, which alone allays longing in love; as to their balsams of life, and essence of pearls, the patient rejected them all; he would hearken to no plan of diet, he conjured the leeches not to plague him, but to allow the sand of his hour-glass to run out quietly, without hastening its pace, by shaking with their officious hands.

For seven long days did secret chagrin gnaw Count Conrad's heart; the roses of his cheeks were all withered; the fire of his eyes was extinguished; the breath of life was suspended between his lips, like a thin morning mist in the valleys, which the slightest gust of wind is capable of dissipating altogether. Matilda had perfect intelligence of everything that was going forward within doors. It was not either from caprice or prudery that she had declined the knight's invitation. It cost her a hard conflict between head and heart – reason and inclination, before she could firmly resolve not to hearken to the call of her beloved. But on the one hand she was desirous of proving the constancy of her fiery suitor, and she hesitated on the other to extort its last wish from the musk-ball: for she considered that a new dress was necessary to the bride; and her godmother had charged her not to lavish away her wishes thoughtlessly. Nevertheless, on the feast day she felt very heavy at heart, retired to a corner, and wept bitterly. The Count's illness, of which she easily divined the cause, gave her still a greater concern; and when she heard of his extreme danger, she was quite inconsolable.

The seventh day, according to the prognostication of the physicians, was to determine for life or death. We may easily conjecture that Matilda voted in favour of her beloved; that she might be instrumental in his recovery was a very probable conjecture, only she could not devise any method of bringing forward her services. However, among the thousand talents which love imparts or unfolds, that of invention is included. In the morning Matilda waited as usual, upon the housekeeper, to receive her instructions respecting the bill of fare. But old Gertrude was in too deep tribulation to be capable of arranging the simplest matter, much less could she regulate the important affair of dinner. Big tears rolled down her leathern cheeks: 'Ah! Matilda,' she sobbed, 'our good master will not live out the day.' These were gloomy tidings: the young lady was ready to sink for sorrow; she soon, however, recovered her spirits, and said, 'Do not despair of our lord's life, he will not die, but recover; this night I have dreamed a good dream.' Old Gertrude was a living repository of dreams: she hunted out every dream of the servants and whenever she could seize one, imagined an interpretation that depended on herself only to fulfil; for the most agreeable dreams in her system boded nothing but squabbles and scolding. 'Let me hear thy dream, that I may interpret it,' said she. – 'I thought,' replied Matilda, 'that I was at home with my mother, she took me aside, and taught me how to prepare a broth from nine sorts of herbs, which cures all sickness, if you do but take three spoonfuls. Prepare this broth for thy master, and he will not die, but get better from the hour he shall eat of it.' Gertrude, much struck at the relation of this dream refraining for the present from all allegorical interpretations. — 'Thy dream,' said she, 'is too extraordinary to have come by chance. Go, this instant, and make ready thy broth, and I will try if I cannot prevail on our lord to taste it.'

Sir Conrad lay feeble, motionless, and immersed in meditations upon his departure hence: he was desirous of receiving the sacrament of extreme unction. In this situation Gertrude entered into his chamber, and by the suppleness of her tongue soon turned aside his thoughts from the contemplation of the four last things. In order to deliver himself from the torment of her well-meant loquacity, he was fain to promise whatever she desired. Meanwhile Matilda prepared an excellent restorative soup, with all sorts of garden herbs and costly spices, and when she had dished it, she dropped the diamond ring, given her by the knight as a pledge of constancy, into the basin, and then bade the servant to carry it up.

The patient so much dreaded the housekeeper's boisterous eloquence, which still echoed in his ears, that he constrained himself to swallow a couple of spoonfuls. In stirring his mess to the bottom he felt a hard body, which could have no business there. He fished it out with the spoon, and beheld, to his astonishment, his own diamond ring. His eye immediately beamed life and youthful fire; his pale, deathly countenance cleared up: to the great satisfaction of Gertrude, and the servants in waiting, he emptied the whole basin, with visible signs of a good appetite. They all ascribed this happy change to the soup for the knight had taken care to keep his ring concealed from the bystanders. He now turned to Gertrude, and inquired, 'Who prepared this good soup for me, that restores my strength, and calls me back to life?' The motherly dame wished the reviving patient to keep himself still, and by no means to exert himself in speaking, she therefore replied, 'Do not give yourself any concern, good sir knight, about the person who prepared the soup: God be praised that it has had the good effect for which all of us prayed!' This evasion was not likely to satisfy the Count: he gravely insisted on an answer to his question, when the housekeeper gave him this information: 'There is a young gipsy servant in the kitchen, she understands the virtues of every herb and plant, it was she who prepared the soup that has done you so much good.' 'Bring her to me this moment,' resumed the knight, 'that I may thank and recompense her for the life she has saved.' 'Pardon me, I beseech you, Sir,' returned Gertrude, 'but the very sight of her would make you ill again. She is as ugly as a toad; her clothes are black and greasy; her hands and face are bedaubed with soot and ashes.' 'Do as I order you,' concluded the Count, 'and let me hear no longer demurs.' Old Gertrude obeyed in silence: she summoned Matilda quickly from the kitchen, and threw over her shoulders her own veil, which she wore at mass, and ushered her, thus caparisoned, into the sick chamber. The knight gave orders that everyone should retire, and shut the door close. He then addressed the gipsy, 'You must acknowledge freely, my girl, how you came by the ring I found in the basin in which my breakfast was served up.' 'Noble knight,' replied the damsel, 'I received the ring out of your own hands: you presented it to me the second evening we danced together at the public rejoicings, it was when you vowed eternal love and constancy to me. – Look now, and say whether my figure or station deserves that on my account you should sink into an early grave. In compassion for the condition to which you were reduced, I could no longer suffer you to remain in such a mistake.'

Count Conrad's weak stomach was not prepared for so strong an antidote to love; he surveyed her some moments in astonishment, and paused. But his imagination soon presented the idea of his charming partner, with whom he by no means reconcile the contrast before his eyes. He naturally conceived a suspicion, that his amour had been betrayed, and his friends were practising a pious fraud to extricate him. Still, however, the genuine ring was proof positive that the beautiful stranger was some way or other concerned in the plot. He therefore determined to cross-examine and convict her out of her own mouth: 'If you are indeed,' said he, 'the lovely maiden to whom I devoted my heart, be assured that I am ready to fulfil my engagement; but take care how you attempt to impose upon me. Reassume but the form under which you appeared two successive nights at the ballroom; make your body taper and straight like a young pine; strip off your scaly skin, like the snake; and like the cameleon change your colour; and the words which I uttered when I delivered this ring to you shall be sacred and inviolable. But if you cannot perform these requisitions, I shall cause you to be corrected for a vile impostor and a thief, unless you satisfy me how you gained possession of this ring.' – 'Alas!' replied Matilda, sighing, 'if it be only the glare of beauty that has dazzled your eyes, woe be to me when time or chance shall rob me of these transient charms; when age shall have spoiled this tender shape, and bowed me down to the ground; when the roses and lilies shall fade, and this sleek skin become shrivelled! When the borrowed form, under which I now appear, shall, as some time it will, belong to me, what will become of your vows and promises?'

Sir Conrad was staggered at this speech, which seemed much too considerate for a kitchen wench. 'Know,' he replied, 'that beauty captivates the heart of man, but virtue alone can retain in the soft bandage of love.' – 'Be it so,' returned the damsel in disguise; 'I go to fulfil your requisitions: the decision of my fate shall be left to your own heart.'

Sir Conrad fluctuated between hope and the dread of a new deception: he called old Gertrude to him, and gave her strict orders: – 'Attend this girl to her chamber, and wait at the door while she puts on her clean clothes. Be sure you do not stir till she comes out.' Old Gertrude took her prisoner under charge, without being able to guess the intention of her lord's injunctions. As they were going upstairs, she inquired, 'If thou hast any fine clothes, why dost thou never shew them to me? But if thou has no change, follow me to my chamber, and I will lend thee what thou needest.' Here upon she went through the whole inventory of her old fashioned wardrobe, by the help of which she had made conquests half a century ago. As she reckoned them up, article by article, a gleam of recollection of past days darted upon her mind. Matilda took little notice of her catalogue: she only asked for a bit of soap and a handful of bran, took up a wash-hand basin, entered her attic, and shut the door, while the new-appointed duenna watched on the outside with all the punctuality that had been recommended to her.

The knight, big with expectation, quitted his bed, put on his most elegant suit, and betook himself to his drawing-room, there to abide the final issue of his love adventure. His impatience made the time seem long, and under his uncertainty he paced quickly up and down the room. Just as the finger of the Italian clock on the Augspurg town hall pointed to eighteen o'clock, the hour of midday, the folding doors flew open of a sudden; the train of a silk negligee rustled along the antichamber: Matilda, arrayed like a bride, and beautiful as the Goddess of Love, stepped into the room. Sir Conrad exclaimed, in the transport of a lover intoxicated with joy, 'Goddess or mortal! whichsoever you may be, behold me prostrate at your feet, ready to renew the vows I have already made, and to confirm them by the most solemn oaths, provided you do not disdain to receive this hand and heart.'

The lady modestly raised the suppliant knight: 'Gently, sir knight, I pray: do not be too rash with your vows; you behold me here in my right shape, but in all other respects I am an utter stranger to you. Many a man has been deceived by a smooth face. You have still the ring on your finger.' Sir Conrad instantly drew it off, and it sparkled on his partner's hand, and she resigned herself to the knight. 'Hence-forward,' she said, 'you are the beloved of my heart. I have no longer any secret for you. I am the daughter of Siegfried the Strong, that stout and honourable knight, whose misfortunes, doubtless, are well know to you. I escaped with difficulty from the downfall of my father's house; and under your roof, though in mean estate, have I found safety and protection.' She proceeded to relate the whole of her story, without even suppressing the mystery of the muskball. Count Conrad, utterly forgetting that he had just been sick to death, invited, for the following day, all the guests who had been driven away by his dejection, before whom he solemnly espoused his bride; and when the server had served up dinner, and counted round, he found that there was no cover too much.

The knight now relinquished the order, and celebrated the marriage with great magnificence. But amid all these important transactions, old Gertrude was totally inactive. The day she kept watch at Matilda's chamber-door, so great was the consternation with which she was seized, at seeing a lady in sumptuous apparel come forth, that she tumbled backward off her seat, dislocated her hip-bone, and limped all her life afterwards.

The new-married couple spent their honeymoon in Augspurg, in mutual happiness and innocent enjoyments, like the first human pair in the garden of Eden. The youthful bride, penetrated by the tender passion, would often recline on her husband's bosom, and pour out the artless dictates of her pure affection. One day, with the most endearing affection, she inquired, 'If you have any latent wish in your breast, impart it to me; I will adopt it, and you shall instantly be gratified. For my own part, the possession of you has left me without anything further to desire; so I shall willingly excuse the musk-ball the wish which is still in reserve.' Count Conrad clasped his affectionate bride fondly in his arms, and firmly protested that he had nothing further to ask for upon earth, except the continuance of their mutual felicity. The musk-ball, therefore, lost all its value in the eyes of its fair possessor, nor had she any motive for preserving it, except a grateful remembrance of her benefactress.

Count Conrad's mother was still living. She passed her widowhood in retirement, at the family seat at Swabeck. Her dutiful daughter-in-law had for some time longed, out of pure filial affection, to beg her blessing, and thank her for the noble son whom she had borne. But the Count always found some pretext for declining the visit; he now proposed, instead, a summer excursion to an estate that had lately fallen to him, and bordered upon the grounds belonging to Siegfried's demolished fortress. Matilda consented with great eagerness. She rejoiced at the idea of revisiting the spot where she had spent her early youth. She explored the ruins of her father's residence; dropped a duteous tear over the ashes of her parents; walked to the Naiad's fountain, and hoped her presence would induce the Nymph to manifest herself. Many a pebble dropped into the spring-head, without the desired effect. Even the musk-ball floated on the surface like an empty bubble, and Matilda herself was fain to be at the trouble of fishing it out again. No Nicksy rose to view, although another christening was at hand; for the lady was on the point of bestowing on her Count one of the blessings of wedlock. She brought forth a boy beautiful as Cupid; and the joy of the parents was so extravagant, that they had almost stifled him with kindness. The mother would never part with him from her arms. She herself watched every breath of the little innocent, although the Count had hired a discreet nurse to attend the infant. But the third night, while all within the castle were buried in profound sleep, after a day of tumultuous rejoicing, and a light slumber had fallen upon the watchful mother, on awaking she found the child vanished out of her arms. She called out in a voice of surprise and terror, 'Nurse! where have you laid my babe?' 'Noble lady,' replied the nurse, 'the dear infant lies in your arms.' The bed and bedchamber were strictly searched, but nothing could be found, except a few spots of blood upon the floor. The nurse, on perceiving this, uttered a loud scream, 'God and all his holy saints have mercy on us! – the Great Griffin has been here, and carried off the child.' The lady pined for the loss of her child, till she became pale and emaciated, and Sir Conrad was inconsolable. Though the belief in the Great Griffin did not weigh a single grain of mustard in his mind, yet, as he could not explain the accident in any plausible manner, he allowed the nurse's prattle free range, and applied himself to comfort his afflicted wife; and she, out of deference to him, who hated all sadness, forced a cheerful countenance.

Time, the assuager of grief, closed by degrees the wound of the mother's heart, and love made up her loss by a second son. Boundless joy for the new heir reigned throughout the palace. The Count feasted with all his neighbours for a whole day's journey round about; the bowl of congratulation passed incessantly from hand to hand; from the lord and his guests to the porter at the door, all drank to the health of the young Count. The anxious mother would not part with the boy; and she resisted the influence of sleep as long as ever her strength would permit. When at last she was not longer able to refuse the call of nature, she took the golden chain from her neck, slung it round the infant's body, and fastened the other end on her own arm: she then crossed herself and the child, that the Great Griffin might have no power to hurt it, and soon after was overtaken by an irresistible slumber. She awoke at the first ray of morning, but – horrible to tell! the sweet babe had vanished out of her arms. In the first alarm she called as before, 'Nurse! where have you laid my infant?' and nurse replied, 'Noble lady, the babe lies in your arms.' Matilda examined the golden chain that was wrapped round her arm; she found that one of the links had been cut through by a pair of sharp scissors, and swooned away at the discovery. The nurse raised an alarm in the house; and Count Conrad, upon hearing what had befallen his lady, drew his knightly sword in a transport of rage and indignation, firmly resolved to inflict condign punishment on the nurse.

'Wretched woman!' he exclaimed in a voice of thunder, 'did I not give thee strict charge to watch all night, and never once to turn aside thine eye from the infant, that when the monster came to rob the sleeping mother, thou mightest raise the house by thy outcries, and scare the Great Griffin away? But thou shalt now sleep an everlasting sleep.'

The woman fell down on her knees before him: 'Yes, my noble lord, I entreat you, as you hope for mercy hereafter, to slay me this instant, that I may carry to the grave the horrid deed mine eyes have seen this night: and which neither rewards nor punishments shall extort from me.' – The Count paused: 'What deed,' he asked, 'have thine eyes beheld this night, too horrid for thy tongue to tell? Better confess, as becomes a faithful servant, than have thy secrets extorted from thee by the rack.' 'Alas!' replied the woman, 'what does your ill-fortune instigate you to force from me! Better the fatal secret were buried with me in the cold ground.' The Count, whose curiosity was only raised the more by suspense, took the woman aside into a private apartment, and by threats and promises forced from her a discovery, which he would fain have been saved the pain of making. 'Your lady, since I must needs disclose it, is a vile sorceress; but she doats without reserve upon you, insomuch that she does not spare even the fruit of her own body to procure the means of preserving your love, and her own beauty unperishable. At the dead of night, when everything was hushed in repose, she feigned herself asleep, and I, without well knowing why, did the same. Not long afterwards she called me by my name, but I took no notice of her proceedings, and feigned to be sound asleep. Supposing me fast asleep, she raised herself upright in her bed, took the infant, and pressing it to her bosom, kissed it fondly, and lisped these words, which I distinctly overheard, "Child of bone, be transformed in to a charm to secure me thy father's love. Now, thou little innocent, go to thy brother, and then I will prepare, from nine sorts of herbs and thy bones, a potent draught, which will perpetuate my beauty and thy father's fondness." – Having said this, she drew a diamond needle out of her hair, forced it through the infant's heart, held the poor innocent out to bleed, and when it had ceased struggling laid it upon the bed before her, took out her musk-ball, and muttered a few words to herself. As she unscrewed the cover, a magic flame blazed forth, and consumed the body in a few moments. She carefully gathered the bones and ashes into a box, which she pushed under the bed. She then, as if suddenly awaking, cried out, "Nurse! what have you done with my babe?" and I replied, shuddering for fear of her sorcery, "Noble lady, the infant lies in your arms." Thereupon she began to shew signs of bitter sorrow, and I ran out of the room, under pretence of calling assistance. – These are the particulars of the horrid deed, which you have forced me to disclose. I am ready to ratify the truth of my words, by suffering the ordeal of carrying a red-hot bar of iron in my naked hands thrice up and down the courtyard.'

Sir Conrad stood as still as though he had been petrified; and it was a long time before he could utter a word. – When he had a little collected himself, he said: 'What occasion is there for the fiery trial? The stamp of truth is impressed on your words; I feel and fully believe that all is as you say. Keep the horrid secret close pent up in your heart. Intrust it to no mortal, not even to the priest when you confess. I will purchase a dispensation from the bishop of Augspurg, so that this sin shall not be imputed to you in this world, nor in that which is to come. I will go in to the hyena with a feigned countenance; and while I embrace her, and speak comfort to her, be sure to draw the box with the dead bones from under the bed, and deliver it secretly to me.'

He stepped into his wife's chamber with the air of a man firm though deeply touched. His lady received him with the eye where no guilt was depicted, though her soul was wounded to death. She did not speak, but her countenance resembled an angel's; the first glance extinguished her husband's rage and madness, for his heart was enflamed by these furious passions. Compassion softened the spirit of vengeance; he clasped the unhappy mother to his bosom, and she moistened his garment with the tears of her affliction. He spoke kind and consoling words to her, but was all the while impatient to quit the scene of abomination. Meantime the nurse had taken care punctually to perform what she was ordered respecting the delivery of the horrid reservoir of bones. It cost his heart a hard struggle before he could determine the fate of the supposed sorceress. He at length resolved to get rid of her privately, and without drawing the notice of mankind towards his domestic grievances. He mounted his steed, and rode away towards Augspurg, after he had given his seneschal these orders, – 'When the Countess, according to the custom of the country, leaves her chamber at the expiration of nine days, for the purpose of bathing, bolt the door on the outside, and let the fires be raised as high as possible, that she may sink under the vehemence of the heat, and come no more out alive.' – The seneschal, who, in common with the whole household, adored his kind and tender-hearted lady, heard these orders with the utmost sorrow and concern. But nevertheless he was afraid to open his lips in opposition to the knight, on account of the positive manner in which he spoke. On the ninth day Matilda gave orders for heating the bath. Her husband, she thought, would not abide long at Augspurg; and she wished, before his return, to eradicate every vestige of her late misfortunes. On entering the bathing-room she observed the air quiver from heat, and she made an effort to retreat, but a vigorous arm forced her irresistibly forwards, and she instantly heard some one without bolt and bar the door. She cried out for help in vain – nobody heard; the fuel was now piled high, and the fire raised, till the furnace glowed like a potter's furnace.

It was not difficult to divine the meaning of all these circumstances. The Countess resigned herself to her fate; only the odious suspicion, which she apprehended had fallen upon her, afflicted her soul much more than her disgraceful death. She took advantage of the last moments of recollection, and drawing a silver pin out of her hair, inscribed these words on the whited wall of the apartment, 'Fare thee well, my Conrad! I die a willing but innocent victim, in consequence of thy commands.' She then threw herself down upon a couch, as her last agonies were approaching. Nature, however, on the approach of the evil hour, will make an involuntary struggle against her dissolution. In the anguish occasioned by the suffocating heat, as the unhappy sufferer tossed and tumbled on the couch, the musk-ball, which she had constantly carried about her, fell to the ground. She snatched it eagerly up, and cried aloud, 'O godmother Naiad, if it be in thy power, deliver me from a dishonourable death, and vindicate my innocence!' She screwed off the top, and the same instant a thick mist arose out of the musk-ball, and diffusing itself through the whole apartment, refreshed the Countess, so that she no longer felt any oppression. The watery vapours from the grotto in the rock had either absorbed the heat, or the kind godmother, in virtue of the antipathy of Naiads to the fiery element, had vanquished her natural enemy. The cloud collected itself into a visible form; and Matilda, whose apprehensions for her life had now vanished, beheld, to her unspeakable joy, the Nymph of the Fountain clasping the new-born infant to her bosom, and holding the elder boy with her right hand.

'Hail, my beloved Matilda!' exclaimed the Naiad: 'happy

was it for thee that thou didst not so heedlessly lavish the third
wish of thy musk-ball as the two former. Behold here the two
living witnesses of thy innocence; they will enable thee to
triumph over the black calumny under which thou hadst nearly
sunk. The inauspicious star that threatened thy life, now rapidly
verges of its decline; henceforward the musk-ball will fulfil no
more of thy wishes; but nothing further remains for thee to
desire; I will unfold the riddle of thy fate; – know, that the
mother of thy husband is the author of all thy calamity. The
marriage of her son proved a dagger to the heart of that proud
woman; who imagined he had stained the honour of his house
by taking a kitchen-wench to his bed. She breathed nothing but
curses and execrations against him, and would no longer acknowledge him for the offspring of her womb. All her thoughts
were bent on contrivances and plots to destroy thee, although
the vigilance of thy husband had hitherto frustrated her malicious designs. She, however at last succeeded to elude his vigilance by means of a fawning, hypocritical nurse. She induced
this woman, by the most liberal promises, to take thy first-born
out of thy arms, whilst asleep, and cast it, like a whelp into the
water. Fortunately she chose my spring-head for her wicked
purpose; and I received the boy in my arms, and have ever since
nursed him as his mother. In the same manner did she un-
designedly commit to my charge the second son of my dear
Matilda. It was this vile deceitful nurse who became thy ac-
cuser. She persuaded the Count that thou wert a sorceress, that a
magic flame had issued from the musk-ball – thou shouldst
have kept thy secret better – in which thou hadst consumed thy
children in order to prepare a love potion from the remains. She
delivered into his hands a box full of the bones of doves and
fowls, which he took for the remains of his children, and, in
consequence of this mistake, gave orders to stifle thee in the
bath. Spurred on by penitence, and an eager desire to counter-
mand this cruel sentence, though he still holds thee guilty, he is
now on his return from Augspurg; and in one short hour thou
wilt recline, with thy honour vindicated, on his bosom.' The
Nymph, having uttered these words, stooped to kiss the Count-

ess's forehead. She then, without waiting for any reply, involved herself in her veil of mist, and was no more seen.

Meanwhile the Count's servants were exerting their utmost efforts to revive the extinguished fire. They thought they could hear the sound of human voices within, whence they concluded that the Countess was still alive. But all their stirring and blowing were ineffectual. The wood would no more take fire than if they had put on a charge of snow-balls. Not long afterwards Count Conrad rode up full speed, and eagerly inquired how it fared with his lady. The servants informed him that they had heated the room right hot, but that the fire went suddenly out, and they supposed that the Countess was yet alive. This intelligence rejoiced his heart. He dismounted, knocked at the door, and called out through the keyhole, 'Art thou alive, Matilda?' And the Countess, hearing her husband's voice, replied, 'Yes, my dear lord, I am alive, and my children are also alive.' Overjoyed at this answer, the impatient Count bade his servants break open the door, the key not being at hand, he rushing into the bathing-room, fell down at the feet of his injured lady, bedewed her unpolluted hands with the tears of repentance, led her and the charming pledges of her innocence and love out of the dreary place of execution to her own apartment, and heard from her own mouth the true account of these transactions. Enraged at the foul calumny and the shameful sacrifice of his infants, he issued orders to apprehend and shut up the treacherous nurse in the bath – The fire now burned kindly, – the chimney roared, – the flames played aloft in the air, – and soon stewed out the diabolical woman's black soul.